Max L. Rosvally

A short Sketch of the Life and Conversion of a Jew

Max L. Rosvally

A short Sketch of the Life and Conversion of a Jew

ISBN/EAN: 9783337148478

Printed in Europe, USA, Canada, Australia, Japan

Cover: Foto ©Raphael Reischuk / pixelio.de

More available books at **www.hansebooks.com**

A Short Sketch

LIFE AND CONVERSION

OF

A JEW.

WRITTEN BY HIMSELF.

New York :
JAMES HUGGINS, PRINTER, 372 PEARL ST.
—
1876.

DEDICATION.

JUNE 6, 1876.

To the Hon. W. E. Dodge.

Dear Sir : I appreciate your great kindness in allowing me to dedicate my little book to yourself.

The philanthropy you possess, and which you so nobly exercise for the benefit of your fellow-men, wins for you the admiration of all persons that are cognizant of your good deeds in the cause of our blessed Lord and Master Jesus Christ.

I know you are anxious to see my book succeed. I pray God that it may prove a lasting blessing wherever it goes, and that its contents may be the good seed sown into good ground, bringing forth a plentiful harvest into the garner of our Lord. This you will greatly help to achieve by allowing yourself to become the godfather of this my first child, and the nurture that it receives thereby will be a guarantee for its future welfare, especially amongst my own people, the Jews ; and if it is the means of leading some of my unbelieving brethren to Jesus the Messiah, it will accomplish the purpose for which it is written.

My prayer to God is that he will ever keep you under the shadow of His wing, guide you through life by His unerring counsel, and that at last you will meet in heaven

THE AUTHOR.

TO THE READER.

·For three reasons I have written this little book:

The first is to show the goodness of God in bringing me from the dark night of Judaism into the marvelous light and love of Jesus; and that the recital of my experience may be the means of bringing many of my brethren, the Jews, to Christ, the despised Nazarene, for a present and a full salvation.

The second reason is, that, taking no pecuniary remuneration from the churches that I visit, I must rely upon the sale of my book for funds to defray my expenses in traveling and working for Jesus.

And my third reason is that I wish to build·a small Tabernacle in the City of New York for converted Jews to worship in.

I have inaugurated meetings in New York City, which are well attended by persons of all denominations, and great good is being done there. My ambition is to erect a House for God without any donations of money, but simply by my own exertions and God's blessing on the work.

I would respectfully suggest that some of my Christian friends should purchase a few copies of my book for gratuitous distribution, especially among the Jews, ·who will read them when given, but will not buy them for themselves.

M. L. R.

RECOMMENDATIONS.

PARSONAGE, Fleet Street, June 1, 1876.

It affords me great pleasure to certify to the zeal and usefulness of Brother Max. L. Rossvally, who addressed our people, much to their profit, on last Sabbath evening. I most heartily commend him to the clergy everywhere, as a most useful evangelist, and as worthy of full confidence.

(Signed)   W. C. STEELE,

Pastor Fleet Street M. E. Church, Brooklyn.

I fully endorse the above.

E. H. GRAY, D.D.

WASHINGTON, D. C.

From Rev. Charles Little.

HACKETTSTOWN, N. J., June 5, 1876.

Having listened with much pleasure to the experience of M. L. Rossvally, a converted Jew, I most heartily commend his pamphlet, "A Short Sketch of the Life and Conversion of a Jew," to the public, and hope the book will be very much blessed by the Holy Spirit in leading many to the Lord Jesus Christ.

PREFACE.

To my Dear Readers:

A friend recently asked me if I was going to preach at Keyport, New Jersey. My answer to him was an anecdote that Mr. RANCOUR told me, and perhaps will not be out of place if I give it here: "There was an old Indian, named Jim, at a country tavern, whose occupation might be termed general usefulness. After a lapse of ten years, a gentleman happened again to stop at this house, and saw the same old Jim there. 'Well, Jim, are you about yet?' asked the gentleman. 'What on earth are you doing nowadays for a living?' 'Well, I don't know,' answered Jim, 'I cut wood, fetch water, hold horses for strangers, make a fire in lawyer Bingham's office, and sometimes *I preach.*' 'Preach, ha! How much do you get for preaching?' 'A shilling,' says Jim. 'Well, now, don't you think that is poor pay?' '*Yes, but it is poor preach.*'"

I am not a preacher, and I am not a lecturer. My story I tell to my fellow-creatures to win them, if possible, to the dear Saviour I have found. The happiness which I feel, I want to make known, that others may have a feast of the spiritual food that I enjoy. My dear reader, will you assist me to spread the glad tidings that are contained in this little book?

After reading it, will you lend it to your friend ? It may be the grain of seed sown in the good ground, and be the means of bringing some soul to the garner of our Lord. "He that winneth souls, is wise." What Jesus has done for me, a wicked, unbelieving Israelite, He will do for all who will accept Him as their Saviour. If this book is the means of bringing only one soul to Christ, it will not be "poor preach." Wonderful are the effects produced on a person by a kind word, a loving smile, or a friendly recognition. These things are not "poor preach," but the true essence of goodness. Let us help each other onward in our journey to the better land. We are ever going forward, either in good works or evil deeds. We are either exalting Christ, or we are denying Him. Do not let your example be against Him, but " Let your light so shine before men, that they may see *your* good works, and glorify your Father which is in heaven." Take Him as your guiding star.

"The beacon burns brightly if we only look to it,
The night may be dark, but our Saviour will guide.
The storms in their fury will drive us close to it,
And there safely anchor'd, we may ever abide."

My prayer to God is, my dear reader, that you will read this book prayerfully, and if it leads you nearer to that brightly burning beacon that diffuses its light over the benighted souls of men, it will not be written in vain.

M. L. R.

New York, May 10th, 1876.

INDEX.

A CONVERTED JEW,

or,

THE NIGHT AND THE MORNING.

From the wilds of Judea, there came forth a stranger,
　All filthy and torn were the clothes that he wore ;
He told a sad tale that his life was in danger,
　And the marks of his grief on his visage he bore.

His full heart sank low, as he thought on his sadness,
　Of no hope for the future, no gain from the past,
And his brain in a fever was yielding to madness,
　As dark visions were passing terrific and fast.

Footsore and dejected he sat by the way,
　No friend had the stranger to welcome him home,
And through the dark night in that place he did stay
　And mourn o'er his sorrows, an outcast alone.

Restless he lay while the storm-wraith was shrieking,
　And fierce was the blast in its sweep o'er the hill ;
His couch on the ground with the rain-fall was reeking,
　And his limbs were disjointed and stiff with the chill.

Sad was his fate in that desolate region,
  And harsh were the sounds that his pain'd ear did
    greet;
No refuge he found in his people's religion,
  For Sinai's thunderings would make him retreat.

Ah! where can a sinner find a covert secure,
  To hide his doom'd head from the force of the blast?
The deep sense of conviction he cannot endure,
  Without help from on high, till its fury is past.

Anon, the black clouds in their pathway were riven,
  And brightly one star gleamed away in the sky;
The dawn of the morning the darkness had driven,
  And the howl of the tempest before it did fly.

And Nature, exhausted, was peacefully resting,
  For a calm had now fell where the storm-wraith
    had been;
No more were dark visions the stranger molesting,
  And tranquil he sat as he gazed on the scene.

His heart swell'd with joy as the glad birds were singing,
  And his face wore a smile that it knew not before;
The flowers on the air their perfume were flinging,
  And he resolved to go back to Judea no more.

Oh! dark is the soul when the sin-wraith is raging,
  And relentless the strife when conviction is there,
Till faith in the Saviour its sorrow assuaging,
  And takes the cleansed heart from the depths of
    despair.

NARRATIVE.

My Early Life.

I was born at Wurtemberg, in Germany, on the 17th day of August, 1828. My father was a merchant in the general dry-goods trade, was of fair standing with his townspeople, a strict observer of the Mosaic law, and the first officer of the synagogue which belonged to the orthodox Jews of that place.

At a very early age, I was taught to curse the name of Jesus Christ, and to spit upon a statue or picture that represented Him, and was told that He was the illegitimate child of a lewd woman.

At school I learned to read the "Torah," or the five books of Moses, in Hebrew and German, and was also taught the French language.

In America, there are a great many Jews that cannot read Hebrew. Recently I attended a mission room, in Baxter Street, New York City, conducted by a young German lady.

There were about forty Jewish children present who could not read or translate Hebrew into English. They were taught by their parents to say prayers in Hebrew, but did not know the meaning of the words they used.

At the age of fourteen years, I went to an academy to prepare myself for entering the University of Hiedelberg, and there I graduated a Doctor of Medicine. But here my early training showed itself. My father had taught me to drink wine when I was very young, and here I drank freely of wine and lager-beer, which proved a great curse to me, and I became a slave to this vicious appetite. But thanks be to God, He has taken away that desire, and now I have not the least appetite for those poisonous compounds.

Whilst under my father's jurisdiction, I had to attend the synagogue three times a day, and was severely punished if I neglected to place any portion of the *Phylacteries* or *Frontlets* on my arms or forehead. Neither did I, while at the University, forget the rites imposed upon me by him. The efficacy of those things, as affecting the salvation of my soul, I never thought of. It was the religion of my fathers, and I was content therewith. I never forgot to kiss the "*Messusah*," on passing through a door-way. But this I must explain to my readers. On the right hand side of the doors, fastened to the wall, is a small tin box about four inches long, one inch wide and half an inch deep, containing a piece of parchment with writing on it, and on this little box there is a face about the size of a one cent coin ; this piece of parchment every orthodox Jew kisses on entering or leaving a room. These things I now look upon as the greatest folly, and wonder why people in this enlightened age can adhere to those ancient rites. But the dawning of a brighter day is shedding its life-giving beams over the Children of Israel, who are flocking to the standard of the cross, and finding there their own Messiah.

I was engaged twice to be married to a Jewess, but the Lord, in His providence, saw fit to frustrate these arrangements. In 1850 or '51, I had been traveling in this country, and on my return to my father's house, my parents wished me to marry a young woman of their acquaintance. My father went to the lady's father to trade for his daughter. Negotiations were entered into, according to the custom of our people, and my father stipulated that for the sum of five thousand florins paid to me, I should marry the young woman. 3,500 florins were offered and refused, but at last 4,500 florins was the sum agreed upon, and I went to visit my affianced bride. But picture my dismay, when I found her to be a most illiterate creature. She had received no education whatever, and her manners were extremely coarse. I could not possibly take a wife of that character after having seen the refined and beautiful ladies of

America, and consequently I left my childhood's home again. My second attempt at matrimony was in Kentucky, but as I was destined not to marry into Judaism, this engagement was also broken off, and I married a young lady of French descent, and of the Roman Catholic faith. Here, also, I had obstacles to surmount, before I could be married. The priest would not perform the ceremony until I promised, that if we had children, they should be baptised and brought up in the Roman Catholic church, and that I would not interfere with my wife in her attendance at mass, or the other services of the church.

At that time it did not matter to me to what church we went; I was quite willing, at all times, to give them any help I could in their performances, and to behave as a respectable citizen should do while there. The Virgin I could gaze on without thinking of her impurity, and could view the image of the infant Jesus without spitting upon it, or troubling my head about his illegitimacy. I became of some use in the services of the church, by joining in the singing of the Te Deum or the Gloria Excelsis, as the case might be. These things were not unnoticed by the priest, who thought to make a proselyte of me, and asked me to become a Roman Catholic. But my answer was, "How can I believe in your religion, with its mummeries, when I do not believe my own, with its ancient traditions?" But God, in His infinite mercy, was reserving me for better things than the blood of bulls, and of goats, and the ashes of an heifer, or the absolutions of priestcraft. It was to be the regeneration of my soul in the precious blood of Jesus, and the forgiveness of my sins through His atonement.

For many years I practiced as a physician, in this country, and when the civil war broke out, I was commissioned as a surgeon in the United States Volunteers, and served as such during the war. While there, I had many opportunities of seeing the effect of christianity on men in the hour of danger and death. At that time, the Rev. Mr. M. Pierce, Chaplain of one of the New York Regiments, would frequently talk to me on the subject of religion, and urge me to become a Christian. I would listen to him patiently, and admire his consistency.

On the field, after the battle of the Wilderness, one evening, in front of the regimental hospital, a captain of the same regiment, and an infidel, who denied the existence of God, invited me to play a game of dominoes with him. The stakes were these : if I won the game, I was to have his share of Christ, and if he won it, he was to take all my Moses and his own Christ. It so happened that I won the game, and gave him back his Christ. While we were playing, the chaplain came by, and we told him what the stakes were that we were playing for. He lifted his eyes in silent prayer for awhile, and then began to pray for us both, that our blasphemy might be forgiven. The captain, crestfallen, cast his eyes on the ground, and I involuntarily let the dominoes fall from my hands. ·This pains my heart to tell it, but it shows my utter depravity at that time.

I have seen, on many of the fields of battle, soldiers die in a most wretched condition, some with curses on their lips, and others I have seen pass away to the better world rejoicing in a Saviour's love, and before their last moment arrived, they have taken from their pockets a Bible, and other religious books, requesting them to be sent to their friends, with their farewell prayers for them.

One soldier in particular, whose limb I was amputating, would not allow me to put him under the influence of chloroform, but just before he died, sang sweetly, "I'm going home to die no more," and his face shone with an inexpressible radiance, as he fell asleep in Jesus; he was a true soldier of the Redeemer. At that time these things made a slight impression upon me, but their influence soon passed away ; still I could not doubt the reality of the Christian religion. The most lasting impressions made upon my mind at that time, were by some Eastern State soldiers, who were convalescent at the hospital of which I had charge ; they would come and bring their Bibles with them, and ask me to join them in prayer ; this sometimes had a great effect upon me, and often brought tears into my eyes, which was only momentary, as the sympathy I felt was not for Christ, but with the soldiers. The great blessings I have experienced since that time, I might have enjoyed then, had my rebellious heart yielded, and accepted the offers of pardon so freely held out to me. It is a mercy indeed that the Holy Spirit of God, who so often strove with me, and whom I resisted again and again, did not take his everlasting flight from me, and leave me to my wickedness ; surely I am a monument of divine grace, and the long-suffering of God has been wonderfully exhibited to me. About the close of the war, I was sent by General Sheridan, to Galveston, Texas, in charge of one of the yellow fever hospitals. At that place, I saw officers and soldiers die by scores. This sometimes had a great effect upon me, especially when the chaplains were ministering consolation to the sufferers, and pointing them to Christ, the Saviour of the world ; the tears would flow freely down my cheeks, so that I could not disguise my emotion ; but like a person determined on his ruin, I always tried to stifle that feeling by drinking brandy or whiskey, and so I went on drinking every day. Still I was not a confirmed drunkard, but that was not my fault, for spirituous liquors had lost their effect upon me, and I could drink enough to make two ordinary men drunk without being intoxicated. I have taken pledge after pledge, that I would drink no more ;

sometimes I would abstain for a week, and
sometimes two weeks, and then drink harder
than ever. My wife often begged me to give
up drinking, and to form a resolution not to
drink, and adhere to it. I promised her I
would do so, but my promises were quickly
broken, and when I did abstain, the prostra-
tion arising therefrom was so great, that she
would advise me to take a little brandy, to
give tone to my system, and stop my nervous-
ness, but thanks be to God, that appetite is all
taken away from me now.

At this rate I was going to perdition as fast
as time could take me. On the night of the
9th February, 1876, a dear Christian man, Mr.
Charles E. Rancour, of Albany, a Superintend-
ent of a Sabbath School and Mission, invited
me to come to the Mission room, to sing. I went
there, and during the service, he asked the
friends present to pray for me, that I might
become a Christian, as I was going away South.
After the service was ended, Mr. R. stood in
front of the Delavan House with me, knowing
the time I was to leave Albany, and there we remained, from two to three hours, in the most
intense cold, with the thermometer below zero;
I was nearly frozen, yet he held me spell-bound,
while he told me of the love of Christ, and of
His willingness to save even the vilest of sinners, and of the efficacy of His blood, that
cleanses from all sin, and all who believe in
Christ will enjoy a present salvation. I thought

if this stranger would work like this for Christ, on such a night, there must be something real in Christianity. At that time I could not realize it, but now, day and night, I would gladly work for the same Master. Working for Him is more than my meat and drink.

The words that the dear brother spoke to me rang in my ears, and are still ringing there, and will ring through all eternity. He wished me good-bye, and with tears in his eyes, he tightly grasped my hand, pressed it with true brotherly love, and said : "I am going to pray for you, that you may find in Jesus the same precious Saviour I have found, before you reach Washington." I have often thought why it is that I love dear brother Rancour so much. Well, I must say, I love him far more than any brother I have in the flesh. Perhaps the Christians who read this will understand it, when I tell them that this man put me in the way to find Jesus, who loved me even unto death. Then why should I not love him, when I so love the one he introduced me to ? He is never contented unless he is working for Christ.

All the way to New York City, and from there to Philadelphia, and from Philadelphia to Baltimore, there was an unaccountable vacancy which the world could not supply. It was my hungering soul seeking food, that alone could be satisfied with the bread of life. On my arrival at Washington, I happened to pick up a newspaper, and the first thing that met my eye, was a notice of a revival meeting, conducted by the Rev. E. P. Hammond, the revivalist, and Mr. Bendley, to be held that evening. A prompting voice constrained me to go to the Congregational Church, Dr. Rankin, Pastor. There I heard Mr. Hammond preach. During the service I could not forget Mr. Rancour's words, as they came rolling through my mind. Tears of contrition flowed from my eyes. I tried to restrain them, but they would not stop. I did not use my pocket-handkerchief, fearing to draw attention to my emotion, and my tears came faster, as the fountain of my eyes was in sympathy with my lacerated heart, and I knew not what to do.

" Oh where can a sinner find a covenant secure,
  To hide his doomed head from the force of the blast ?
The deep sense of conviction, he cannot endure,
  Without help from on high, till its fury is past."

I determined to leave the Church, and drown my convictions in brandy. As I reached the door, going out, my attention was arrested by the singing of " Jesus of Nazareth passeth by." This was the Jesus I was longing to find, but my rebellious heart would not yield to Him. At that moment a Christian lady, Mrs. Young, who had been watching me, came and caught me by the coat, and asked me if I was going away ? "Don't you see I am ?" I said. " Well you must not go, I want to speak with you. " She requested me to sit by her

side, and she knelt down and prayed for me.
I felt a dreadful choking sensation, as if my
heart was bursting. I remember having felt
such a sensation once before, on leaving my
dear mother, when I tried to say good-bye to
her, but the words could not find utterance.
After a while I left the Church, with a full de-
termination of taking some brandy to drive
away these feelings. I got in front of a rum
shop, but there was a strange restraining power
that prevented me going into it, and held me
back so that I could not get inside. I went home
to my own room, closed the door, turned off
the gas, and there, in a corner, fell on my knees,
for the first time in my life, I addressed myself
direct to Jesus, and I prayed.

"Oh! Lord, Jesus Christ, if thou art the Messiah that I am looking for—if thou art the
Saviour of mankind—reveal thyself to me this
night. Take away this darkness, and enlighten
my mind, and let me feel that peace and consolation that thy children feel. Take away this
terrible appetite and evil passion, and I will
serve thee while I live. Hear my prayer, oh!
Lord, Jesus, and cleanse my soul from sin, for
thy dear name's sake."

OH, LEAVE ME NOT ALONE.

My life is filled with sad regrets;
　No peace attends my way;
Each day the sun in darkness sets.
　Oh, hear me, Lord, I pray. _

OH, LEAVE ME NOT ALONE.

Words and Music by M. L. R.

1. My life is filled with sad re-grets; No peace at-tends my way;

Each day the sun in dark-ness sets, Oh, hear me, Lord, I pray.

Oh, let me not in dark-ness rove, But melt my heart of stone;

Ac - cept my faint attempts at love, And fix my heart on things above;

"Come Ho - ly Spir - it, heaven-ly Dove," Oh, leave me not a - lone,

"Come Ho - ly Spir - it, heavenly Dove," Oh, leave me not a - lone.

Oh, let me not in darkness rove,
    But melt my heart of stone ;
Accept my faint attempts at love,
And fix my heart on things above ;
" Come Holy Spirit, heavenly dove,"
    Oh, leave me not alone.

Indulgent God of love and power,
    To Thee for help I fly ;
Be with me at this solemn hour,
    And hear my contrite sigh.
Renew my heart and be my guide
    To Thy celestial throne ;
Oh, let me see Thy wounded side ;
I come to Thee, the crucified ;
Lord, condescend to be my guide,
    Oh, leave me not alone.

My heart with inward horror shrinks ;
    I feel this load of sin ;
Far from the shadow of Thy wings,
    All darkness is within.
Now take me, Lord, into Thy care,
    And melt my heart of stone.
My load is more than I can bear,
And Thou didst not disdain to hear
The publican, in fervent prayer ;
    Oh, leave me not alone.

I know Thou canst not let me go,
    Thy blood for me was shed :
Now let me sink beneath its flow,
    And raise me from the dead,
And bid me stretch my withered arm
    To Thee, whose love is shown,
And grasp Thy mantle, with its charm
To take from death its dread alarm,
And then, reclining on Thine arm,
    I shall not be alone.

For about two hours and a half, I was on
my knees and bed alternately, and could no}
sleep, and though that night was exceedingly
cold, and no fire in my room, yet drops of sweat
poured over me, as if I had been placed before
a heated furnace; my breast felt as if I was
screwed in a vise, until half-past 2 o'clock
Saturday morning.

At last, light, glorious light illumined my
benighted soul, and I was filled with joy, and
love, and peace. I became a new creature in
Christ Jesus. I went into the street to proclaim
the joyful tidings, and though I breathed the
same air, ate the same food, and wore the same
clothes, yet everything seemed changed and
new to me. I wanted to shake hands with everybody, and make everybody feel as I felt. I was
not contented to have all this happiness alone;
I wanted others to share it with me.

The second day after I found Jesus, the Rev.
Mr. Hammond wanted some out-of-door meetings held, and for that purpose he got on horse-
back and rode to the corner of Pennsylvania
Avenue and Seventh Street. There we procured
a dry goods box; Mr. H. addressed the people
from his horse; we sang two or three hymns,
offered prayer, and invited the people to come
to Lincoln Hall, where the morning meetings
were held. This was on Monday. That evening,
at the Congregational Church, Mr. Hammond
invited me to take charge of the out-of-door
meeting. Next morning, I accordingly (on

Tuesday A. M.) went to the aforesaid place, and there found the dry goods box. At eleven o'clock, the hour appointed for the meeting, I mounted the box. There was no person near, but a boot-black, and to him I gave five cents, to stand there and listen to me. I commenced my service by singing "Jesus lover of my soul," and before I got through with the second verse I had about 300 persons around me, many of whom were Jews. When they heard me say that I had found the Messiah, they laughed at and scoffed at me ; they said that I was a fool, was crazy, and a fanatic, and that I was paid for coming there. Had some one, four or five days before that time, offered me all the money in the Treasury of Washington to stand up and face an audience of that kind in a public street, with a dry goods box for a pulpit, I could not have done it ; but thanks be to my blessed Master, who gave to Saul of Tarsus power to proclaim the unsearchable riches of Christ, who before his conversion, had been a great persecutor and blasphemer, this same Jesus gave to me the requisite strength to speak to that assembly of Jews and Gentiles. I said to them, if to love and serve such a precious Saviour as mine is fanaticism, then I am a fanatic ; and I prayed that all who heard me that morning, and I pray that all who may read this book, may become the subjects of a like fanaticism. And as for my being paid, thank God, no one goes into His vineyard without receiving an ample and a lasting reward. The promises to his servants are sure and steadfast : " Lo, I am with with you alway, even unto the end of the world." "Thy bread shall be given thee, and thy water shall be sure." "Be thou faithful unto death, and I will give thee a crown of life." And then comes the great *pay day :* "Come, ye blessed of my Father, inherit the Kingdom prepared for you from before the foundation of the world."

If the preaching of Christ to degraded sinners be fanaticism, this fanaticism shall be my greatest boast, and my rejoicing all the day. Oh, may it show itself in my intercourse with men, and ever dwell upon my tongue! I do not wonder at men of the world, who know nothing of the blessed change that takes place in a man when the Holy Spirit takes possession of his heart, and he shows the wonderful transformation that has passed over him, setting him down as a fanatic, a fool, and as being crazy. No one can understand the new birth until it is experienced. The joy is such as was not realized before ; the vicious temper is subdued, and the meekness of the lamb takes its place ; the vulture becomes a dove. To myself, before I received the blessing of forgiveness, it was a problem I could not solve, and often wondered what the strange power could be, that showed its influence so lovingly in Christians ; but now, glory be to God, I know it by experience, having passed from death unto life. I am willing to be counted a fanatic, while I am permitted to unfold the glorious truths of the Gospel of Christ, and a fool, while I have such rich supplies of heavenly wisdom, and crazy, while I have Jesus for my Great Physician, my brother, and my guide.

About four or five days after my conversion, I-met, at the Baltimore & Ohio depot, a Mr. B., a young man about 23 years of age. He was trying to get into a carriage while in a state of drunkenness. I noticed that he had got his foot on a spoke of a wheel instead of the step. I went up to him and said, "Can I speak to you, my young friend?" at the same time removing his foot from the carriage. He turned around, looked me in the face, and asked if I was a Catholic Priest. I replied, "I am not." "Are you a Methodist preacher?" "No, I am not." "Then who to h— are you?" "I am your friend," I said, "will you let me speak with you?" He said, "Come and have a drink." I said "Not to-day." I saw the young man was determined to get away from me, so I followed him from about half-past nine A. M. to four P. M., and during that time he drank at least fifteen glasses of rum and ale. At last I succeeded in following him home, where I found his mother, a widow of one of the most respectable families in Washington, who, on account of her son's drunkenness, had left the neighborhood where they formerly resided, and moved to another locality, to keep from being disgraced or disgracing her boy. I could not do much with the young man that evening in the state he was in, and I told his mother I would call the next morning and see them. On the following morning I found him sober; his head was swollen, his eyes were protruding from their sockets, and, as all drinkers know, to their sorrow, his stomach was in a dreadful state. I talked with him a while and got him interested in the conversation, when a feeling came over me, and I thought I ought to pray with him. I knelt in front of him, took him by the lappels of his coat, and gently drew him on his knees in front of me, and there in the presence of his mother, I asked God, for the sake of his Son Jesus Christ, to take away the appetite for strong drink from this young man, as He had done from me. For several days I visited him two or three times a day, and always prayed with him, and in the mean time, asked all the Christian people to pray for him. On the fourth day, after offering prayer, *Mr. B.* said to me, "If you, Mr. R., a stranger, take so much interest in me, it is about time that I should take some interest in myself."

That evening he went with me to hear Mr. Hammond preach, and was converted that same night. He is now a good and faithful worker for Jesus. The appetite for drink is taken from him, and he is giving daily experience of his acceptance with Christ. Surely this is "a brand plucked from the burning."

Since I left Washington, I have received letters of a very cheering character from him, and he is so zealous in the cause of Christ, that when Mr. Hammond left for Baltimore, my young friend went there to relate his experience, that other young men might profit by it and be saved. The case of the young man here given, is not an isolated one; there are tens of thousands of persons who are treading on the verge of eternal perdition, and who are dead in trespasses and sins, without having any desire beyond the accumulation of this world's goods, or the gratification of their sensual appetites. They are spiritually dead to "the things that make for their peace," and move about on this earth without thinking of a future life. The drunkard seeks to drown the voice of the Spirit by his libations, and sears his conscience by blasphemy and revelling in his cups, until he goes down to the grave, and to eternal ruin. His name is soon forgotten by his boon companions, but his deathless soul is undergoing the tortures of the lost.

Reader, allow me to ask you, is your heart dead to "the things that make for your peace?" Are you rejecting the offers of life, eternal life? That life that can alone be had by coming to Christ, who is the fountain of life, and of love, and who is the bright and the morning star to dispel the darkness from your mind and take away your carnal propensities. It is the glorious sunlight of righteousness, that must

warm and cheer and elevate our cold hearts
into the newness of life, and raise us from the
death of sin. But there is something for us to
do ; we must "seek the Lord while He may be
found, and call upon Him while He is near,"
and be willing to give up everything that hin-
ders our coming to Christ. We must be willing
to be nothing in our own estimation, that we
may receive Christ, the only Saviour, and be
willing to become as a little child, before we can
grow up to the stature of men, in Christ Jesus.

We are dead in trespasses and sin, and without the quickening power of the Spirit we shall
remain lifeless like a withered tree, without
bud, without leaf, and without fruit, only cum-
berers of the ground, without peace here, or
hope hereafter. Did we possess a lease of our
lives, and know the hour we should leave this
world, would it not be folly to trifle away our
precious moments? How much greater folly
is it, when we have not a minute to call our own,
to be reckless about the salvation of our immortal souls ! "We think all men mortal but
ourselves."

Like a surgeon in a military hospital, after a
hard fought battle, looks on the writhings of
the wounded soldiers without a tremor, and
hears their heart-rending cries without sympathy, so is it with man. Our finer feelings
are blunted by sin and mixing up with the
people of the world ; our character, in a great
measure, is formed by evil companions.

My dear reader, if your besetting sin is drunkenness, ask God to take away the appetite that
you have for strong drink. Jesus is the physician of the body as well as the soul ; there is
no disease so inveterate, as to be beyond His
skill to cure. He took that craven desire from
me. I used to tremble like an aspen leaf, when
I saw the picture of a glass of ale with its foam-
ing head painted on a sign board, and the devil
would suggest to me, to go around, and get in
by a back door. The testimony of thousands of
reclaimed drunkards is, that Jesus is able to
save to the uttermost, all that come unto Him,
and remember this : "No drunkard shall inherit the Kingdom of Heaven." .

After my conversion, I was so anxious to
work for Christ, that I went into the enquiry
room every day and night, whenever and
wherever I could. It was about the 9th day of
March, I said to a young man in the enquiry
room of the Congregational Church at Washington, "My friend, are you a Christian? do
you love Jesus?" He replied, "I don't want
any man to talk to me about Jesus, especially
a Jew," and with that he threw his hat in my
face. This cut me to the very soul, and I said
to him, "My friend, if you had done that two
months ago, before my conversion, and I had a
pistol with me, I should have put a bullet
through you ; now I want to show you what
that Jesus has done for me." I handed the
young man his hat, saying to him, "My friend,

you need praying for, I am going to pray for you." The manner I acted towards him completely subdued him, for he came to me in five minutes afterwards, and said he was sorry for what he had done; "I ought not to have thrown my hat in your face; I ask your pardon." I told him, he should ask Jesus for pardon, for it was Him he had insulted. I at once turned round to the congregation and shouted as loudly as possible, "I ask every Christian in this house (there being about 2,500 people present) to pray for a young man who has thrown his hat in my face, for asking him if he loves Jesus." The next day, at the Calvary Baptist Church, when Mr. Hammond held his morning prayer meeting, I again asked the prayers of God's people for that same young man, and I prayed for him daily, at every meeting.

On the evening of the twelfth day, Mrs. Young, the same dear Christian lady who caught me by the coat, showed me a young lady in whom she felt a deep interest, and asked me to speak to her. I went and spoke to her, and she said to me, "Speak to my brother," and made room for me to sit between them. The young man was the person who threw his hat in my face. I asked them "if they were willing for me to pray with them?" The young man reached his hand forth to me, and began to cry, and both him and his sister knelt for prayer, and in less than fifteen minutes, they were rejoicing in the Lord Jesus.

Oh! how my soul was filled with gratitude
to God, and my heart leapt for gladness! I
thanked Him that the hat was thrown in my
face, for it was the means of bringing that sinner to himself. There is no more interesting
place to me, than the enquiry room of a religious meeting. There we see human nature in its
various phases; the refined and the vulgar
meet there; the learned and the illiterate mingle
their prayers; the virtuous and the abandoned
come there for the same purpose, to see Jesus;
the silvery haired disciple, who has borne the
heat and the burden of the day, infuses courage
into the newly born convert, and gives him
counsel how to proceed along the narrow pathway that leads to heaven. There the overcharged
heart unburthens its sorrow, and lays it all at
the foot of the cross; the drunkard and the
thief confess their sins and find pardon and
peace: there a mother supplicates for a beloved
child, and a child prays for a wicked father;
and there loved ones are remembered, though
far away, and petitions ascend to the throne of
heavenly grace for blessings to come down
upon them; and there luke-warm Christians
learn that loiterers in the Church are stumbling
blocks, in the way of others, and are impelled
forward more vigorously to do battle for the
Lord: there the formalist finds himself
weighed in the balances and found wanting,
and that his religion is of no value without
Christ, and then we feel that the religion of

Christ is a vital, life-giving, soul-inspiring reality.

I fell in love with the good people in Washington; and I can never forget the many kindnesses I received from them. But where everyone was so good, it would be invidious to mention names in particular; suffice it to say, that I made more friends there in a few days, than I had done in all the 46 years of my life before, and I had determined to settle down with the dear friends who cared so much for my soul, because I found my Saviour there.

Business matters compelled me to visit New York, and on my arrival in that city, I went to the Hippodrome, to hear Mr. Moody preach. And speedily I went to work, with all my soul, in the enquiry room; for Mr. Hammond had so engrafted the spirit of it into my heart, that I would hold an enquiry meeting with myself in the railway cars, when alone. At the Hippodrome there was a wide field opened up to me. Hundreds of persons came there daily, seeking salvation, and asking for sympathy and consolation. How my heart yearned over these poor creatures! Many of them seemed to be the offscouring of the earth, and the marks of poverty and suffering were deeply engraven on their faces.

A large number of the men that came there were drunkards. Many drank because they had the demon craving for it; others drank to allay sorrow, but found that " wine is a mocker." With these people I worked heartily. Knowing my own sad besetment, I could talk to them experimentally on that subject. And I told them, "that it was the drunkard and outcast of society, that my Lord and Master came to save." And to give those poor creatures a word of consolation, and point them to the Saviour, was my delight.

I was greatly impressed by the assemblage at the Hippodrome. Looking at that sea of faces as I sat on the platform, I felt inspired with awe, as I thought on the assembled world meeting before Him "that sitteth on the Great White Throne." There, in that meeting, the dark race of Africa was stretching forth their hands to God, the Jew was seeking the Messiah, and the various nationalities were seeking one common Saviour. Truly, "The same Lord over all is rich, unto all that call upon Him." The singing of those beautiful hymns by Mr. Sankey, and the refrain by that vast assembly, was wonderfully effective. It seemed to me at times as if one part of the hymn would be taken up by a thousand voices, and another portion in the opposite part of the house, and would waft the sweet cadence from one to the other; it was truly thrilling, it seemed heavenly. But what struck me most, was the power Mr. Moody possessed over his audience in arresting and sustaining their attention, which shows there is something more at work there, than mere human agency. Truly, excitement may have somewhat to do with bringing the masses together, for human nature is such that notoriety is sought after, and no doubt many persons visited the Hippodrome to see Mr. Moody personally. The success of his preaching lay in his earnestness, and believing in what he said, and therefore, like a good workman, he did his work well. His manner is energetic, which carries force with it, and gives it weight. He is a true Bible scholar, as his well thumbed Bible testifies. He turns to any verse required with a facility that shows that he knows exactly where to find it; and being gifted with a good memory, he intersperses his addresses with anecdotes, with telling effect. He appears not to forget anything that comes under his notice, and reserves the incident for future use.

Theology, as taught in the schools, does not trouble him much. He preaches Christ, as the Saviour of the world, who is ready to give a full, free, and present salvation to every one that will accept it. Mr. Moody's religion is of a decided practical character, that admits of no trifling. It is, "*Now* is the accepted time. Behold! *now* is the day of salvation." Procrastination is not only the thief of time, but has allured thousands of souls to hell. On Sabbath afternoon, I went to Jerry McCauley's mission, in Water Street, New York. And I would advise all my readers, when in this city, to pay a visit to "The Helping Hand." It is very encouraging to know that the number of persons who attend there is so large, that a more spacious building is necessary, to accommodate them. Mr. McCauley is very pointed in his manner of addressing his hearers, and very strict in enforcing the rules laid down there. The assembly is composed largely of sea-faring men, in their ordinary working attire. On one occasion, after prayer, and a portion of the Scripture was read, he said, "Remember the minute rule. I used to work for a man, and I used to sneak off and go one side and steal time. What do you think I was doing? I was stowing away, smoking an old pipe; that was stealing time. Now don't you know that when we take things that don't belong to us, we are stealing? When we take time belonging to others, it is stealing. Remember particularly the minute rule. Sometimes my wife touches the organ, and that is a hint for me to sit down. I am not a prophet, nor the son of a prophet, but I prophesy that we are going to have a good time to-night. It depends on us whether we will or not. The meeting is open. If you young converts would stand up and speak, you would enjoy the meeting wonderfully. You will have the 'blues' all through the meeting if you don't get up and say, that Jesus has saved you." This address is characteristic of the man. He wins his hearers by becoming one with them.

A man arose, and said : "I thank God, Christ

has saved me ; I forgot that blessed Saviour for
forty years, and twenty years of that time I
was a drunkard. I asked Him a thousand
times to damn my soul. I never thought to bow
my knee in prayer to God who made me. I
used to make up my mind I would drink no
more, and then I would get drunk. I kept on
this way year after year. I came here three or
four nights. I began to think ; that is a small
word, THINK, but there is a world of meaning
in it. I thought I had not asked God to help
me. I went on my knees and asked God ; the
first time I had been on my knees to my Saviour for forty years. That blessed Saviour
heard that prayer, crooked as it was. He took
it and laid it at His Father's feet, and I bless
God, that first prayer was answered. When I
got up next morning, instead of going out for
bitters, I thanked God for what He had done for
my soul. Since that time, there has been no
Sabbath-breaking and drinking for me. I am
now 57 years of age ; what would I not give if
I could recall that forty years of my life ! But
I can't do it." Two or three others having
spoken a few words, Jerry McCauley said,
"Now we will have a prayer meeting for those
who feel their need of the prayers of God's
people. It seems to me, every unsaved person
can be saved here to-night, if he WILL, at this
meeting. I call this meeting a FAILURE, I
call every meeting a FAILURE, if no one is
converted. Christ's people can get together

and shout, and all that sort of thing, but if no
one is saved, what does it amount to? Blessed
be God, every night for four years, I have had
prayer. Rum halls are kept open every night,
and Sunday night too. They don't care about
your excise law. Your Commissioners don't
care much either. They go home and go to
sleep, and you might as well take a chair and
sit down, as go to see one of them. I came
near wearing a pair of shoes out, going to see
them. What you say to them, goes in at one
ear and out of the other. I believe in a religion
that will save men from every kind of sin.
Some persons say 'Brother McCauley is a little
fanatical ; he is too hard on a sinner.' He is not
hard enough. Oh! I tell you the time will come
when your cry will be, 'Oh! that I only lived
nearer to God, and that I was a better Christian!'
I tell you, dear friends, that Jesus gives us a
PERFECT salvation, but we make it imperfect
ourselves. I believe, that if Christian people
lived right, there would be such a mighty
power in this city, it would tremble from one
part to the other, and people would say, 'God
is here of a truth.' I have seen men tremble,
and hide their heads under the benches, as an
old woman cried out, 'I see Him! He is coming!'
I have known men to run out, and slam that
door. Why? Because the Spirit of God con-
victed them of sin, and they ran away from it.
God cannot do any more than what He is doing.
The Holy Ghost is drawing you, and pleading

with you, and you are resisting Him.   Do you
want to be saved to-night ?   Some people would
not lift up their hand to be saved ; they are
stubborn.   Oh, my God, help some soul to be
willing here to be saved to-night !   Let God
take the pride out of your hearts.   Are you
proud that you have a good coat, or a few
greenbacks, or a *gold watch ?*   Humble yourself before God.   Some people will not kneel
down to these old benches ; they say, ' I want
a cushion, I do ; when I want to be converted,
I want to go to some fancy place ; this place is
good enough for them old fellows down there.'
I tell you, unless you get down like us poor
fellows, God never will save you.   You must
do it in your heart.   It will not make any
difference whether you have a cushion or an
old rotten bench.   You must be humble, like
a little child.   I feel there is unbelief here.
Oh, may God take it out of every heart !"

I was much struck by the appearance of a
remarkable looking woman, who arose and
said : "Two years ago, I thank God, my child's
little dress, that I had washed and hung out of
the window to dry, was blown over into Mrs.
McCauley's yard ; that circumstance was the
means of bringing me to Christ.   I had been a
drunkard and a strumpet for years, walking the
streets of New York.   I did everything that
was bad.   I would hire a child, and squeeze it
and starve it, to make it look sickly, to beg.
My husband was a sailor, and a drunkard like

myself. We had to sleep on the floor, from the fact that when we had a quilt or blanket, I would take it to the pawn-shop, and for two or three days would go without bread, and drinking all the time.

When my husband came home from sea, we would go on a spree, and drink until every cent was spent. As I said before, the little frock flew into Mrs. McCauley's yard, and I went after it. I asked her if I could go into the yard for it, and she said 'Certainly.' From my appearance, Mrs. McCauley must have thought what I was, for my dress was very dirty and ragged, my hair was not combed, and I looked filthy. Mrs. McCauley asked me what I was doing for a living. I told her 'Nothing in particular.' She said, 'You come for your child's dress ; there are people that come here, and look for something that they least expect, but, thanks be to the Lord, they find it. Won't you come ? We have meetings here.' 'Well,' I said to her, 'I have not a piece of bread to eat, and your Jesus ain't a going to give it to me.' 'I will give you some in the name of Jesus,' said Mrs. McC., and she gave me two loaves of bread. That kindness made such an impression on me, that on that evening I went to the meeting ; but it was more because I had no fire in my room, and I wanted to warm myself. I began to feel interested, and I kept coming to this meeting, and thanks be to the Lord, I found the Saviour here, and he

has taken away all the appetite for drink.
Friends, if you will come to my room, you will
find there now such furniture as a working-
man can afford. I have George Washington's
picture, and the pictures of General Jackson
and Generals Lee and Beauregard, on my walls,
and I can now spare a few shillings a month,
for missionary work, and can give a poor woman a dinner or a supper. My husband, who
sits here by me, is a dear, darling, sober man ;
he don't go to sea no more ; he earns his 12 or
14 dollars a week, and I earn 5 or 6, and we
save up a little money. On my last birthday,
he made me a present of a nice Bible. Jesus
will do for any of you what he has done for me.
Instead of my husband fighting and pulling my
hair, we sit and have family worship."

I sat and looked at that man and woman with
surprise. I wanted to rise and speak, as the impression they made upon me was so great, but
every time I arose, two men would pull me
down, and when I did gain the floor, I had to
observe Jerry McCauley's rule, and all I said
was "May God bless you !" I could see the
love of Christ beaming in that woman's face,
for it was radiant, and her husband shed tears
of joy all the time she was speaking. That
woman and her husband had been prayed for
hundreds of times, and it was in answer to
prayer, God wrought this wonderful change.

Another instance of the wonderful power of
prayer came under my notice recently. A

young gentleman purchased tickets for himself and sister for a ball, that was to be held in the town. In the evening when they were dressing themselves to attend the ball, their mother, a wealthy lady and a good Christian, remonstrated with them on the folly of their going to such a place, when most young folks were going to Church, and said to them, "You ought not to go to a ball, my children." The reply of the young man was, that he had paid $2.50 for the tickets, and had promised to attend. The mother said, "Henry and Helen, if you persist in going to the ball to-night, I will go on my knees, and remain there until you return, and pray God to have mercy on you."

The young lady and her brother left their home with the full purpose of going to the ball room. When passing by the doors of a church in which a revival meeting was being held, the young lady's attention was attracted by the singing, and she asked her brother to go inside with her, if only for one minute. They came in, and were seated, when the lady drew my attention, and I left the platform, and entered into conversation with them. When the revivalist asked that such persons as desired the prayers of the Christian people should rise, both brother and sister stood up. The time for which they entered was prolonged into an hour, and again lengthened until they found their Saviour. The young man took the tickets for the ball from his pocket and showed them in the meeting. We may expect that those ball dresses will become more beautiful in the eyes of those young people, as they will remember under what circumstances they were worn, and the results arising from prayer. This occurrence transpired on the 25th day of April last, in a town on the Mohawk River. On the 5th of May, I met the young gentleman at the noonday prayer meeting in Fulton St., New York, and we rejoiced to meet each other. I refrain from giving names, by request.

At one of these meetings, I met a man 74 years of age ; his hair was white as snow, and his silvery beard came down over his breast, giving him a patriarchal appearance. He arose in the meeting and told how he had found Christ just nine days before. Think of it : that old man, only nine days a child of God ! He had been the captain of a slave ship, and on different voyages from Africa, when chased by British cruisers, he had thrown 286 human beings overboard into the sea. For forty-nine years he had not been in a church ; though he knew there was a God, yet he did not believe in Him. On the 2d day of April, 1876, he came home, and quietly went to his daughter's room, having left her unwell that morning. When he reached the top of the stairs, he heard his daughter's voice, and on opening the door softly he found her on on her knees, with her head resting on the table, and her hands clasped, supplicating the Throne of Grace for her father's salvation. Her prayer was : "Oh, Lord Jesus, save my father; I cannot live and see him thus ; he is my father ; though his sins are many, and of the blackest kind, yet dear Jesus, as Thou did'st forgive the thief on the cross, Thou canst forgive him.   Oh ! dear Saviour, save him now !   Hear my supplication, oh, God !"   The old man could stand it no longer.   He went from the door and fell flat on the floor.   And his daughter seeing it, fell across him, with her arms around his neck, crying out, " Lord Jesus, give me my father ; give him light to see his need of Thee."   For about twenty minutes, both remained silent on the floor, and when she aroused him, and looked at his face, she said, "Dear father, do look in the glass ; you look a different man."   And surely he was a different man, for the trans-forming power of God had cleansed him, and made him a new creature in Christ Jesus.   Well might the old man's knees tremble, as he told at the meeting of the wonderful condescension of God, and of the mighty power of faithful prayer.   He met with a friend in his old age, whom he derided and insulted in his younger days.   We cannot think of a more desperate and blasphemous character, than the captain of a slave ship, lost to all sense of sympathetic feeling.   They delight in rapine and cruelty. We think from the nature of their calling, they cannot be far removed from demons.   And yet this man, at the age of 74 years, when we would have thought his heart was seared by crime, so that nothing could reclaim him, came under the influence of the love of Jesus, and budded, and brought forth fruit to the glory of His name. His conversion and communion with Jesus, must be surpassingly sweet to him.

A LITTLE TALK WITH JESUS.

" A little talk with Jesus; how it smooths the rugged
    road ;
How it seems to help me onward, when I faint beneath
    my load ;
When my heart is crush'd with sorrow, and my eyes
    with tears are dim,
There's naught can yield me comfort, like a little talk
    with Him.

I tell Him I am weary, and I fain would be at rest;
That I am daily, hourly longing for a home upon
    His breast ;
And He answers me so sweetly, in tones of tenderest love,
' I am coming soon to take thee to my happy home
    above.'

Ah! this is what I'm wanting, His lovely face to see ;
And, I'm not afraid to say it, I know He's wanting me ;
He gave His life a ransom, to make me all His own,
And He can't forget His promise to me, His purchased
    one.

I know the way is dreary to yonder far-off clime,
But a little talk with Jesus will while away the time ;
And yet the more I know Him, and all His grace
    explore,
It only sets me longing to know Him more and more.

I cannot live without Him, nor would I if I could ;
He is my daily portion, my medicine, my food ;
He's altogether lovely, none can with Him compare ;
The chief among ten thousand, the fairest of the fair.

So I'll wait a little longer, till His appointed time,
And glory in the knowledge that such a hope is mine;
Then in my Father's dwelling, where many mansions be,
I'll sweetly talk with Jesus, and He shall talk with me."

While at Little Falls, I stopped at the house Mrs. Voskburgh, and one day she requested me to go in to see her mother, as the old lady wanted the converted Jew (meaning myself) to pray with her. I went into her room, and found an *aged Christian* there, 93 years of age, who had been following Jesus 79 years. She was busily engaged making a patch-work quilt. I took her by the hand ; knelt in front of her, and began to sing my favorite hymn, "Jesus lover of my soul, let me to Thy bosom fly." She being deaf, I had to place my mouth close to her ear, and she placed her head on my shoulder, and with one hand stroking my head, as if she were blessing me. Oh ! how I felt, I cannot describe. My heart shrank within me, to see that old lady, who had followed Jesus for so long a period as 79 years, and myself comparatively only a few days His child, after denying Him for forty-six years. I prayed with her, and bade her good night.

The following morning she sent for me to repeat the same service, after which she sang "I am coming, Lord, to Thee," in a very low, hardly perceptible voice. Yet I thought it was the sweetest music I had ever heard. On that morning, she requested me to kneel, to receive

her blessing. It was very gratifying for me to
receive her benediction. And may I prove as
faithful to my Lord and Master as this, His
aged handmaiden, who has borne the heat and
the burden of the day, and who is patiently
waiting to be summoned to meet Him in heaven.

After breakfast, the Rev. Mr. Patterson, the
revivalist, invited me to climb the mountain
that overhangs the city of Little Falls, in search
of crystals (by some persons called diamonds)
that are found there.   When on the mountain
top, overlooking the city and the falls of the
Mohawk River, we were sitting down ; I took
out my Testament and read, and said, "Christ
preached on the mountain and prayed on the
mountain." Then Mr. Patterson said, "Let
us do likewise." We then commenced a prayer
meeting, and the beautiful feathered tribe joined
us in singing the praises of our Great Immanuel.
It seemed as if we were at the gate of heaven,
and enjoying the peaceful serenity of that city,
whose builder and maker is God. Away from
the busy haunts of man, we were holding sweet
communion with our Saviour, as it were, ele-
vated between earth and the home of the just
men made perfect. And under the blue etherial
canopy of heaven, our souls were being feasted
with a fresh manifestation of our Saviour's love,
to prepare us for going forth, to proclaim the
glad tidings of a present salvation. Our blessed,
Master would often go up on the mountain to
pray, and we, His followers, imitating His ex-

ample, met with Him there. There in seclusion
our minds were not distracted, but feeling like
His disciples felt, on the Mount of Transfigur-
ation, we were ready to exclaim, "Lord, let us
make three tabernacles here ; one for Thee, and
one for Moses, and one for Elias!" But He
requires the tabernacles of our heart, which we
gladly give Him.

On our way back to the city, when crossing
the Erie canal, we saw a blind man, feeling his
way with a stick to come off the steps. Mr.
Patterson and myself shook hands with him,
and said, "Good morning friend, can you come
to-night to our revival meeting, and hear a converted Jew give his experience?" said Mr. P.
"Oh! that's you, Mr. Patterson? I heard you
preach the other night. I know you by your
voice. And your sermon done me a heap of
good. I have been serving my Master for many
years, and, though I am blind, I see Him by
faith every day." That dear blind man came
that night, and fairly shouted when I spoke of
the love of Jesus.

"I have far sweeter communion with Jesus,"
said a blind man, in an experience meeting,
"since I lost my sight, than I ever had before.
Now I can sit and think on Him, and talk with
Him, more than I used to do. And He comes
nearer me, as if to recompense me for the loss
of my eyesight. But my spiritual vision is
clearer and brighter, and I am longing to go
home, to see the King in His beauty, and see

that glorious city, the new Jerusalem, to sweep
the golden lyre and sing the new song. To
Him that loved us, and washed us in His own
blood, and hath made us kings and priests
unto God, to Him be glory and dominion for
ever and ever, amen. I am longing to go home.
I could leave my wife and my children, for
Jesus will take care of them.

> " For me my elder brethren stay,
>   And angels beckon me away,
>   And Jesus bids me come."

At. the same place, the following evening,
two young men came there to disturb the meeting, and brought with them, in their pockets,
small torpedoes or *balls*, that explode with a
loud noise when thrown on the ground. These
were intended to be thrown among the people
when rising for prayer ; but the restraining
hand of God was upon these young men, and
the arrow of conviction entered the heart of one
of them. He became a seeker for pardon, and
after a while found peace. This young man,
after the sermon, was the first to arise for
prayer. He put his hand into his pocket, and
took the torpedoes therefrom, and with his face
covered by his handkerchief, and crying, he
told how he intended to disturb the meeting
with them.

For a person to doubt the efficacy of prayer,
is to deny the goodness of God. Do we suppose for a moment, that man was created and
left to his own resources, without adequate

means given to him for producing the necessaries that he requires to sustain his existence, when we had such overwhelming proof of it on every hand? There was provision made for his physical sustenance, that by the sweat of his face he should eat bread. He goes forth to his labor; he breaks up the ground, he ploughs the soil, he prepares it, and then sows the seed in it, and waits patiently in faith, for he cannot hasten its growth. After a while the sprouting blade shows itself, and imperceptibly grows, and expands until the ear shows itself, and then the full corn in the ear, and at last the golden grain is ready for the sickle. My readers perhaps will say, "Yes, I knew all this before." But, did you ever think over it, to see what analogy there is between the sowing of the seed, and the offering of your prayers? The seed is sown in prepared ground. The prayers are offered from regenerated hearts. In the natural course of events, you know that harvest time will come. So surely will the prayer of faith be answered. We pay too much attention to worldly matters; too often forgetting that there is a higher life, a nobler manhood, to which we should aspire; an aspiration that is only worth living for, and for which we are sent into this world. There is a strange fatality hanging over man, that constantly keeps him in a state of perplexity, and he knows no peace until he comes to Jesus for it. He says, "My peace I give unto you; not as the world giveth, give l unto you." It is lasting peace ; but we must seek for it, and we must trust in Jesus, for it. God has made ample provision for our spiritual, as well as our temporal necessities. I sometimes think how foolish it is to argue this matter, when everything around us proves the goodness of God towards us. But this strange fatality, *sin*, corrodes the souls of men, and warps their reason, and soothes them by its sophistry, and syren-like, lulls them into false security. My dear reader, if you are being lulled by the syren song of sin, try the prayer of blind Bartimeus : "Jesus, Thou son of David, have mercy on me." And it will be your own fault if your spiritual vision is not healed from the blinding effects of sin, and you do not see Jesus as the one altogether lovely.

Let me tell you where God answered my prayer on the spot. I was at the town of Keyport, in the State of New Jersey, one Sabbath day, and, after the evening service, at a church there, we held an enquiry meeting. It was something that was never held there before. The minister requested all Christians to rise, and about one-half of the congregation stood up. He then asked all those who desired to be Christians, to stand up, but no one arose. He then requested me to take charge of the meeting, and I asked if there were any young men present, who desired the prayers of their Christian friends, to stand up. I repeated the question two or three times, still no one arose. I found that to be the coldest meeting I had been in, since my conversion. It seemed as if the congregation were seated on an *iceberg*, in the *Arctic Ocean*. It made me feel very bad indeed. I saw I could do nothing in front of the people, so I made a flank movement, and attacked them in the rear. There I asked a dozen young men to rise for prayer, but all refused. I felt discouraged for awhile, but God, having repeatedly answered my prayers, I thought I would appeal to Him again. So I knelt down in the aisle, and with as loud a voice as I could command, cried out: "Oh, my Lord Jesus Christ! Thou who art ever ready to hear and answer prayer. I ask Thee to put it into the heart of one young man, at least, to rise for prayer. And Jesus, Thy name shall have all glory." I had not said amen, before the young man I first spoke to, and who had positively refused to rise, fell on his knees by my side, and, instead of me putting my arms around his neck, as I am accustomed to do, he put his · arms around mine, and with tears flowing from his eyes, said : "Do pray for me." My heart was filled with thankfulness to God. I arose, and requested all Christians who did not feel in sympathy with this seeking sinner, to leave the church, and all the young men who wished to become Christians, and desired prayers, should stay behind, and I would remain all night, if need be, and pray with them. The Rev. Mr.

Mead, the Pastor of the Church, myself, and a converted Jewess, with two or three of the Christian workers, remained there until nearly twelve o'clock at night. Four young men remained; two were converted. And still the good work is going on, and souls are being brought to Christ.

I have inaugurated in New York City, meetings for converted Jews. The following, I copy from the *New York Daily Witness:*

"A GOOD WORK AMONG THE CHOSEN PEOPLE.— A religious meeting was held on Tuesday afternoon, at 69 Second Avenue, corner of Fourth Street, presided over by a converted Israelite, from Washington, D. C., who has been in New York City, Albany and elsewhere, successfully working in the vineyard of Christ. The object of this meeting, was to form a union, to be called 'The Hebrew Christian Association.' Its members to be converted Jews, who will hold their meetings one evening weekly, to which all Israelites are cordially invited. The meeting on Tuesday was a successful one. There were about sixty persons present, many of whom had recently found the Saviour, and were ready to testify to the power and willingness of Jesus to save sinners, and to go forth among their brethren to tell them what God had done for their souls. It is hoped that the meeting on Tuesday will be the nucleus for extending more fully the missionary spirit of converted Jews, and we hope for great results therefrom. We are glad to notice that many young Jews and Jewesses are deciding for Christ, and it is interesting to hear them relate their experience in our meetings. There are upwards of 200 converted Jews in New York City. These alone would form a noble band of workers to unfold the blood stained banner of the cross."

Our second meeting was held on the evening of Friday, the 5th of May, in Hope Chapel, at the corner of Avenue C and Fourth Street. Four young Jews arose and told the meeting of the great love of Christ, as experienced by them. One young man, who has been driven from his home for giving his heart to Jesus, and is persecuted by his people, offered prayer, full of love and confidence and hope ; and as he said, "When my father and mother forsake me, then the Lord will take me up," he made an effective appeal to all present, and their prayers, with his, were presented at the throne of grace.

There is something extremely interesting in hearing these young Jews talking of Christ, apart from the prejudice that envelopes their race, and more so, as conversions among the Jews occur so seldom, simply because so very little is done for their spiritual welfare. The church, in this land, has held itself aloof from them, and have treated them as a stiff-necked, stubborn race. Stubborn and stiff-necked they are, and they will become more so, but Christians should be delighted to labor contentedly in the field our dear Lord commanded us to cultivate. And He will surely bless our efforts, if we sow beside all waters.

One dear sister, a converted Jewess, arose and said : "When I was a child, my father sold pictures, and some of those pictures were representations of Jesus ; he sold them because he wanted the money ; and we used to spit upon them, and if the frame of one was broken, we would take the picture up and throw it away. And when I went out to work, I lived with Roman Catholic people, and they had Jesus hung up against the wall, and I would go and point at it in derision. But when I began to read about Christ, I thought this man surely was a good man, and I went to church with these people. But that did not satisfy me ; I wanted something else. And I looked at the picture on the cross, and that did not satisfy me ; I wanted something more. And I went to mass, but that would not do ; I wanted something more. And I began to pray to Jesus, and He filled my heart with *love*. And when my brother came to see me, I told him he could come there, but that I was a Christian, and that Jesus was not on the wall merely, but I had Him in my heart, and glory be to His holy name, He is there now, and He remains with me. He is a dear, good friend. He has been with me ever since I knew Him. Glory to His holy name ! I love to tell of His goodness, and what He has done for me. Glory to His holy name ! And my dear friends, He will do the same for you. He will never leave you. He will never forsake you. He has been with me through sickness and sorrow, and when my people abused me, for His sake, I did not care for that, for He is my Saviour, and my friend, and all my hope is in Him. For He has promised to take me to heaven at last.''

Testimonies like these require no comment. They tell their own tale, and carry conviction with them. They show that our Jesus is "a friend that sticketh closer than a brother." That without Him, there is an empty void the world can never fill, but that all fullness dwells in Him. How cheering to the weary traveler, passing through this wilderness world, to hear Him say, "Lo, I am with you alway, even unto the end of the world." Guiding us through all our troubles; guarding us in every danger; never leaving us, never forsaking us.

Let me give you the experience of another dear sister, a lady of this city, Esther King, who was disowned by her family, Jews, for becoming a Christian. Perhaps it may interest some of our young readers, if I give it in verse:

" They frown, that once had smiled on her,
  A floweret of their ancient tribe ;
Her name is spoken with a slur,
  Her spotless fame they now deride.

No longer hers, her childhood's home
  Has pass'd to others of her race,
And now, a wanderer, she roams,
  To seek herself a resting-place.

And cold the winter's wind did blow,
  While onward was her fearless tread,
And deeply lay the fallen snow,
  When from her childhood's home she fled.

But heeding not the stormy blast,
  Nor shrinking from their withering frown,
The threshold of that home she pass'd,
  Resolved to win the victor's crown,

And follow Him who once had died
   Upon the cross, in Palestine ;
He whom her sires had crucified,
   The curs'd and hated Nazarine.

She saw the rod of Jesse's stem,
   The branch that issued from its root;
It was the babe of Bethlehem,
   The vine that bore the promised fruit.

And the Messiah, she ascribes
   The Shiloh of the olden time,
The Lion of famed Judah's tribe,
   To Jesus Christ, of David's line.

The rose of Sharon bloom'd for her,
   And fair the valley's lily grew ;
The rose with perfume fill'd the air,
   The lily gave its radiance too.

She heeded not the piercing blast ;
   For her, no terrors had the night ;
A sheltering arm 'round her was cast,
   A whisper put her fears to flight.

'Lo, I am with thee,' gave her strength
   To wrestle, in that hour of need ;
She knew that victory at length,
   Would in her favor be decreed.

And soon the morn began to dawn,
   The conflict of the night was o'er ;
Her soul was free, its chain was gone,
   Such joy she never knew before.

The rose of Sharon bloom'd for her,
   And fair the valley's lily grew ;
The rose with perfume fill'd the air,
   The lily gave its radiance too.

She sought the vineyard of her Lord,
   Where laborers she knew were few,
And armed with His eternal word,
   She taught the unbelieving Jew.

She raised the drunkard from the mire,
  Who soon forgot his oaths obscene;
No more a slave to base desire,
  She soothed the fallen Magdalene,

And told them of the crimson flood,
  That washes whiter than the snow;
The riches of the Saviour's blood,
  Its freedom, and its constant flow;

And pointing to her home above;
  The maid of Judah swept her lyre;
She sang of His redeeming love,
  She sang with a seraphic fire.

The seraphs caught the thrilling strain,
  And tried redeeming love to sing;
The song re-echoed o'er the plain,
  It made the heavenly mansions ring.

And far above the seraph choir,
  Was heard the maiden's sweet refrain;
Whene'er she swept the tuneful lyre,
  The blood of Jesus was her strain.

And listening angels gathered round,
  To hear the songstress trill the tale;
Its mystery was too profound
  For angel wisdom to unveil.

'Twas wondrous love to fallen-man,
  That brought Messiah on this earth;
'Twas Godlike to devise the plan,
  That gave to man the second birth,

And born anew, true beauties see
  In what before he did deride,
And joining nature's minstrelsy,
  In praise of Him they crucified.

And Judah's sons are now elate
  With joy, to find the Nazarine,
And hasten to the glorious state,
  With Him who died in Palestine.

The rose of Sharon blooms for them,
And the fair valley's lily grows,
The rose entwines with Jesse's stem,
And Judah's tribe embrace the rose.

And Salem's daughter still proclaims
To scoffing Jew, and drunkard wild,
The open door, that yet remains,
Through Jesus Christ, the Virgin's child.

The *New York Daily Witness* kindly gives the following extract of our second meeting:

"A GOOD WORK AMONG THE CHOSEN PEOPLE.— A religious meeting of the Hebrew Christian Association was held on Friday evening, May 5th, 1876, at Hope Chapel, corner of Avenue C and Fourth Street. There was a good attendance of converted Israelites and other friends. The experience of a converted Jewess made a deep impression on her hearers, and it was pleasant to see so many young Jews arise and tell of the love of Christ towards them, and their faith and confidence in their Saviour.

"The meetings are to be continued in the same, on Friday evenings, until further notice, when all converted Jews are invited to attend and take part in the service. Our friend from Washington, who inaugurated these meetings, still continues busily engaged in the Lord's vineyard, and is doing great good in this city and neighborhood, and under his conduct, these union meetings no doubt will be successful in winning souls to Christ. When so much energy is put forth, great results must follow. We shall watch these meetings with interest, and aid them all we can by our influence and prayers. We ask every Christian to do the same, for the bringing of the children to Christ is a noble work to be engaged in, and all can help by their petitions to the throne of grace."

I purpose, with God's help, to open two or three other places in the City of New York, for this purpose : the bringing of converted Jews, of various denominations, together, and helping each other onward to the heavenly Jerusalem.

There was a beautiful young Jewess at Washington, D. C., who read of my conversion, and the happiness I experienced in the Christian religion. She wrote me a letter, requesting me to meet her at the reading room of the Young Men's Christian Association, at ten o'clock on the next morning. Mr. Hammond read the letter, and told me it would not be proper for me to meet her alone, and asked four or five Christian ladies to do so, with me. At the house where she resided, her intention to meet me became known, and she was detained there, so that she could not keep her appointment. In her letter she gave an account of a man, a Jew, who some thirteen months previously, she had fallen in love with, and at Baltimore, they were, as she supposed, married, but the ceremony was a mock one. They came to Washington, and the man took her to a house of ill fame, representing it to be a private boarding house, and left her there with only thirteen dollars. I went to the house, and took two policemen with me, and demanded her; but the women told us that no such person lived there. In her second letter she said that she was sorry to disappoint us, but that the mistress of the house would be absent on the morrow, and she would then get out and · go to the Baltimore and Ohio depot, and leave Washington for

New York, and there would apply to the Ladies' Christian Aid Society. She told us, she
was tired of leading such a life, and would rather
die than stay where she was. She had never in
her life said a prayer. Thanks be to God, she
fell into the hands of a Christian lady. She is
now truly converted, and is now visiting the
poor, and the sick, and the prisoners, working
for Jesus. I have met her at several religious
meetings in this city. She told me that previ-
ous to her conversion, she premeditated suicide,
and had gone to the river Pótomac for that
purpose. Her parents, at Baltimore, have put
their curse upon her; it is too horrible to pub-
lish here; they consider her as dead.

I have related this, and such like incidents,
at meetings that I have attended; and I have
been told by persons, that religion is greatly
mixed up with excitement. My answer is, "It
may be. But supposing that Mr. A. T. Stew-
art had bequeathed to you, in his will, the sum
of 10,000 dollars, and you never expected such
a thing, would you not feel excited?" "Well,
yes; I should." "How long would that excitement last? Would it last a week?" "Yes,
it would." "Would it last three weeks, or
would it last four weeks?" "I suppose it
would." "Well, when the excitement passed
away, you would still have the 10,000 dollars,
would you not?" "Yes, of course." Well,
my friend, so it is with the love of Christ.
When it is implanted in the heart, there

it remains. If a man loves a woman on the day of their marriage, that love increases the longer they live together. But if there is no love existing between them, then he never loves her. So it is with our love for Jesus. "We love Him, because He first loved us, and gave Himself for a propitiation for us," and we love Him more and more, the closer we get to Him, until He takes us to Himself in heaven.

Supposing there was a poor, filthy, degraded man, one of the worst of human kind, to whom Commodore Vanderbilt gave his check, payable to bearer, for 5,000 dollars, and told him to go to the bank and get the money, and provide himself with decent apparel. The man takes it to the bank, and presents it to the cashier. Do you think the cashier refuses to pay the money because the man's appearance is rough? Certainly not; he knows the signature of Commodore Vanderbilt, and that is all he requires. so it is with our Father in heaven; He is no respecter of persons. The potentates of the earth must come to the same Saviour, and in the same way as the vilest sinner. There is but one way to heaven; and admittance into the celestial city can only be gained by a passport, signed by, and with the shed blood of the crucified Redeemer. It matters not what your lineage or nationality is, the phraseology of your language, or the color of your skin. All are God's children if the sprinkled blood is on the heart. Your raiment may be old and torn,

but He will clothe you in the robe of righteousness. Your speech may be unintelligible, but
He will fill your mouth with songs of praise.
Your friends may deride you, and forsake you,
but angels are your attendants, and your title
is a prince of heaven and Jehovah's son.

In conclusion, let me speak a few words to
my brethren, the Israelites, and ask them no
longer to reject Jesus as the Messiah. He it
was of whom the prophet Isaiah wrote : (Is.
vii : 14 :) "Therefore the Lord himself shall
give you a sign. Behold, a virgin shall con-
ceive and bear a son, and shall call his name
Immanuel." And again : (Is. ix : 6 :) "For
unto us a child is born, unto us a son is given ;
and the government shall be upon his shoulder,
and his name shall be called WONDERFUL
COUNSELLOR, the Mighty God, the Everlasting
Father, the Prince of Peace." Doubtless this
prophecy was fulfilled when the Infant Jesus
was born in Bethlehem. And again the prophecy was repeated by the angel to Joseph : "Behold, a virgin shall be with child, and shall
bring forth a son, and they shall call his name
Emmanuel, which being interpreted is God with
us." And St. Mark tells us that "Jesus came
from Nazareth of Galilee, and was baptised of
John in Jordan, and straightway coming up out
of the water, he saw the heavens opened and
the Spirit, like a dove, descending upon him,
and there came a voice from heaven saying,
'Thou art my beloved Son, in whom I am well

pleased.'" These facts should convince the most obdurate heart, that Jesus is the Son of God. Apart from the writings of Holy Writ, let us take the testimony of thousands of converted Israelites, who are testifying to the faith that was once delivered to the saints, by the love of Jesus filling and warming their hearts. Think what this mysterious power can be, that so alters the nature of men, that changes their very looks, that takes them from the mire and filth of sin, and elevates them to be heirs of God, and joint heirs with Christ Jesus.

Let me ask you, my dear brethren, is there not an emptiness in your hearts, which nothing that you can do supplies? Is there not a small still voice prompting you to seek peace through the blood of the crucified Saviour? Do not the tears often start from your eyes when some serious thought passes through your mind? and you exclaim: "Oh, that I could find Him whom my soul longs to love!" These promptings, and those tears, are the voice of the Holy Spirit, knocking at the door of your hearts, and trying to woo you to himself, and unwilling to leave you. Can you reject the offers of His love? Why will you put off a matter of such vital importance to you? Remember your immortal soul is at stake, which is of more value than ten thousand worlds.

> "If for a world a soul be lost,
>   What can the loss supply?
> More than a thousand worlds it cost,
>   A single soul to buy."

And remember that your souls are immortal, deathless, and will live while eternal ages roll their cycles. This life, like a vapor, passes rapidly away; but short as it is, it is the only time we have to prepare for the eternal world.

This question, my dear brethren, is of too serious a character to be trifled with. The ·skeptic may scoff at the name of Jesus; the blasphemer may blaspheme His name, and the unbelieving Jew may deride Him, but these cannot obliterate the great truth written in God's holy word: "I and my Father are one." And again: "I am the resurrection and the life. He that believeth in Me, though he were dead, yet shall he live, and he that liveth and believeth in Me, shall never die." Jesus will take you just as you are, and cleanse you from all sin and all impurity. The thief on the cross cried unto Him, and was saved; and Jesus said unto him: "To-day shalt thou be with Me in paradise." If the tears of contrition bedim your eyes, check them not, but let them flow.

> "Flow on my sad tears, ever flow,
>   Let your fountains no longer be dry,
> Till Jesus His blood doth bestow,
>   Till my heart to His love doth reply."

The flowing of those tears arises from the softening process of the Holy Spirit, preparing your hearts for the reception of your Saviour's love; love far surpassing that of a devoted mother's; steadfast as the rock of ages, and boundless as eternity. And can you refuse this love, so graciously offered and so generously given? will you not yield to the persuasion of your Saviour? That was first said to the Jews: "Son, give me thine heart." And yielding your heart to Him, He will give you eternal life, a crown of glory, and a victor's palm. There is no preparation required on your part, only believe that Jesus is the Messiah, the Son of God, the Saviour of the world, the Prince of Peace, and accept Him, and you will be saved.

A few years ago, in England, an old sailor was going through the streets of a town there, singing:

> "I am a poor sinner, and nothing at all,
> But Jesus Christ is my all in all."

There was a poor foolish fellow who heard the the sailor singing, and followed him through the streets; his shattered mind grasped the words and retained them. A short time afterwards he was laid on a sick bed, and there he sang:

> "I am a poor sinner, and nothing at all,
> But Jesus Christ is my all in all."

In a few days, he died, rejoicing in a Saviour's love, and his last words were those he heard the old sailor singing in the street. And this must be our case. "Nothing at all."—We have no merit of ourselves; there is no plea we can bring on our own behalf. "Nothing at all."—There is no price to pay for this great salvation, for Jesus paid it all on Calvary; no sacrifice to make, for Jesus was the one great oblation. "Nothing at all," but to come just as we are, for Jesus Christ is all in all.

Would you see the beauty of this Christian character portrayed in all its loveliness, go to the bedside of the languishing sufferer who has lain upon that couch for years, with limbs distorted and withered with disease ; look on that pallid countenance, and observe the peaceful smile, and ask yourself the reason, and see if you can find an answer to your question. The body may be racked by pain and sickness, but the soul filled with the presence of Jesus, feasts on the riches of His grace, and dwells in sweet serenity, awaiting only the dissolution of the clay tenement,

> "To clap its glad wings and soar away,
> And mingle with the blaze of day."

And this unspeakable happiness, my dear brethren, may be yours. Joy unbounded and full of glory. Won't you give your hearts to Jesus ?

> "Come in this moment at His call,
> And live for Him who died for all."

May God bless you, is the prayer of your sincere friend.

M. L. R.

www.ingramcontent.com/pod-product-compliance
Lightning Source LLC
Chambersburg PA
CBHW030026030726
47499CB00008B/3130